THE ORDER OF
THE BULL

by
Phillip Yates

CHAPTER 1

Brian Martin stared out the dusty window of the minivan, hating his life. Single and double-wide trailers covered in mildew and rust flanked both sides of the road like oversized tombstones marking the graves of giants. If ever there was a place where people might go to die, this would be it.

The October County Trailer Court looked like a breeding ground for poverty and desperation. Brian had seen these sorts of places before, but only at a distance and only from the relative safety of the minivan (like a tourist taking a trolley ride through the zoo.) Never once had he considered the possibility that he might actually live in this kind of squalor.

Broken toys, squashed beer cans, ratty Confederate flags, rusted-out lawn mowers, cracked toilets, spare tires, Nascar memorabilia, and an assortment of other junk filled the yards. Dirty-faced kids played outside, oblivious to the lives they had to look forward to. A few haggard men smoked cigarettes and guzzled beer on a front porch that looked on the verge of collapse. They eyed the minivan with distaste, as if they were just as unhappy about this new integration of city and country as the Martins were. Brian wasn't sure such a thing was possible.

The trailer court could have easily been mistaken as a landfill were it not for the scattered signs of life that had been added to give the place some small air of respectability. A well-kept azalea bed here and there. A front porch with a Welcome mat and swing. A child's shiny new bicycle that hadn't yet suffered the same fate as all the other rusty artifacts.

There was something else, however, that seemed neither distinctly Southern nor on par with the rest of the tasteless decorum. Bright orange sun symbols had been painted on the doors of each and every trailer, including the one they were going to call home.

"I think this is the place," Janet Martin said as cheerfully as she could muster under the circumstances.

"Yeah, this is the place...if the place is Hell," Brian grumbled. "Maybe that's the reason for all those spray-painted fireballs. Somehow, I expected Hell to smell like sulfur, but this place just smells like B.O. and weed."

Janet sighed. "This is not my idea of paradise either, kiddo. I didn't choose this life for us."

"No, you didn't," Brian conceded. "Dad chose this for us when he ran off with that whore."

"I promise we'll get our own place as quickly as possible," Janet said. "Just hang in there."

The wasteland ahead looked like the skies had opened up and flooded the world with junk. Brian picked up his phone and started to video everything he saw through the window. "I think I'll document our little stay here," he said. "If that won't build a child abuse case against Dad, then nothing will."

2

He panned the phone's camera from left to right, capturing a pack of stray dogs and some strange yard ornamentation that had been fashioned to resemble the face of Dale Earnhardt. He was just about to zoom in on two of the dogs who were busy fighting over a bag of torn garbage when he caught a glimpse of something out of the corner of his eye. Later, he would swear he had seen a bull standing in the road, right in front of their van.

"Mom, look out," Brian shouted as he panned the phone back, certain they were about to crash into the beast. He had heard stories about people who hit cows that wandered into the road. In most of those stories, the cows were unharmed. The vehicles, on the other hand, were usually totaled.

Janet Martin slammed on her brakes and then shot her son a stern look. "Don't do that!" she said. "You scared me. I see the guy."

When Brian panned the phone back, he realized he must have been mistaken about what he had seen. "Sorry," he muttered.

The man in the road looked nothing like a cow of any sort. Brian realized that his mind must have conjured that image up since cows were about the only backwoods thing missing in this Godforsaken, redneck Mecca. He recognized the man from the porch where all the other hillbillies had their cheeks packed with tobacco and their bloodstreams full of Budweiser. The man had a gleaming steel ring in his nose that looked like a halter for cattle. His torso was covered with an intricate crisscrossing network of white scars. His nipples were pierced and adorned with sterling silver rings that matched the one in his septum. Blue prison tattoos ran the length of both arms. He wore dirty jeans and cowboy boots. His dark hair had been buzzed close to the scalp. His eyes were shrewd and probing.

Strangely enough, he walked over to Brian's side of the van. Brian rolled his window down and studied the man carefully.

"You folks lost?" the man asked, squinting against the sun. Something about the man's shifty demeanor put Brian on edge.

"Nope," Brian replied, trying not to show any discomfort. "We know exactly where we are. It's our first time here in Mayberry."

"Good deal," the man said, oblivious to Brian's sarcasm. He extended his hand through the window. "Name's Dennis Earl Gentry."

Brian shook the man's hand, squeezing hard enough to let Dennis Earl know that he wasn't just some snot-nosed kid. Dennis Earl squeezed back, grinding the bones in Brian's hand. The look in the man's eyes was cold but his mouth remained fixed in a smile. His touch felt like snakeskin, and Brian tried not to let his revulsion show.

"Is there something we can help you with or do you usually stand in the middle of the road for no reason?" Brian asked.

"Brian!" Janet snapped. "Don't be so rude. Sir, I apologize for my son. He didn't mean it."

"Don't worry about that," Dennis Earl replied with a lazy drawl. "Boys will be boys. The only reason I stopped you in the first place is because one of your tires looks like it could use some air."

"You're very kind, Mr. Gentry," Janet said.

"Don't think another thing about it," Dennis Earl said as he moved from the passenger's side of the van to the driver's side. "I was that age once and had a smart mouth myself. Got my hide blistered with an extension cord for

4

it too. But, that was a different day and time. Now, everything is more civilized. When kids talk out of turn, we discuss their feelings and try to reason with them. I seen that on Oprah once. But enough about that. Welcome to the neighborhood, Pretty Lady."

Janet blushed and smiled. At that moment, Brian realized that his mother was like a wayward mouse running toward a python's open mouth. Dennis Earl was every bit a predator and made no attempt to hide his motives.

"I don't believe I've had the pleasure," Dennis Earl said as he toyed with one of his nipple rings.

Janet smiled. "Nice to meet you, Mr. Gentry. I'm Janet Martin. My son and I are moving here. We'll be living in Jack Martin's single-wide."

Dennis Earl's eyes widened a little. "You're Jack's family? We're practically neighbors. I'd be glad to show you around the place whenever you get settled in. Unless you'd rather let your husband get a lay of the land first."

"My husband and I are no longer together," Janet said. Her hands fluttered across the front of her dress like nervous butterflies, unsure where to land. She absently ran a hand through her auburn hair, brushing a strand of it back over one ear.

"That's a shame, ma'am," Dennis Earl said. "If there's ever anything I can do to help you out in any way, just give me a call or send your boy over to my place. I live in the double-wide at the end of the lane."

"The boy and his mother will be fine," Brian interjected.

"I'm sure you will," Dennis Earl grinned. "Don't forget to get that tire checked out, you hear?"

Dennis Earl gave them one final wave goodbye and turned back toward the porch. That's when Brian saw the sun symbol on his left shoulder. It looked identical to the

5

one on all the trailer doors. Only it hadn't been painted on. It wasn't exactly a tattoo either. It looked more like a cattle brand of some sort. The thought of anything related to livestock was enough to remind Brian of what he thought he had seen through the screen of his phone.

Brian pushed the thought out of his mind, still confused about why he had imagined such a thing. The sight of his new home was enough to make him temporarily forget about everything but the depressing downward spiral of his life.

"We're here," his mother announced.

CHAPTER 2

Brian knew without a doubt that the avocado-colored sardine box sitting amidst the waist-high weeds and heaps of worn-out tires was Uncle Jack's trailer. The wrought-iron likeness of Elvis Presley in the front yard assured him of that.

Like all the other units in the trailer court, the door to Uncle Jack's trailer bore the stenciled image of the sun. That image turned out to be an accurate representation of the interior once his mother opened the front door. The heat inside the trailer was stifling, and Brian immediately raced over to the air conditioning unit that was mounted in the window. He turned the switch several times before realizing that the unit didn't work.

"You gotta be kidding," he muttered. "No air?"

"Good thing I brought a box fan," his mother sighed. "Looks like we'll be needing it."

Brian banged his fist on the wall and huffed as he mentally added one more thing to the list of hardships his father had thrust upon them. "I wonder what else doesn't work in this hellhole."

For the most part, the inside of the trailer looked like

a small two-bedroom apartment. Most of the furnish-
ings—like the green shag carpeting in the kitchen and the
cheap wood paneling—were seriously outdated. Still, the
place seemed decent enough. Had he not been able to see
the adjacent trailers through the living room window and
the ragtag heaps of junk in each yard, Brian could have
convinced himself that he was just spending a few nights
in a shabby run-down motel. The incessant yapping of
hunting dogs next door and the distant strains of Hank
Williams Jr, however, made that impossible.

After spending most of the day traveling, neither Brian
nor his mother felt much like unpacking. Brian located the
portable fan buried underneath their luggage in the back
of the van. He plugged it in and turned the speed up as high
as it would go, hoping to stir up enough of a breeze to keep
them cool. Janet crawled onto the couch, kicked off her
shoes, and closed her eyes. Brian fell into the ratty, moth-
eaten recliner and leaned back, hoping to wake up and realize that this was all just a bad dream.

The sun was melting into the west when they dozed
off. When Brian woke up a couple of hours later, someone
was screaming...

Startled, Brian turned on a reading lamp and was surprised to see that his mother was still sound asleep, despite
the noise. Careful not to wake her, he opened the front
door and stepped out into the darkness. Immediately, he
knew that something was wrong. Something snorted and
growled and shrieked like a chained banshee. Curious, he
followed the sounds, eventually arriving at a dilapidated
shed in the nearby woods.

Strange barnyard smells of wet hay and offal
blanketed the shack, giving rise to a storm cloud of flies
and mosquitoes. Brian swatted the bugs away and put his

hand over his mouth to keep out some of the stench. He nearly screamed when he heard a sound that resembled the lowing of cattle. Although he managed to keep himself under control, all he could think about was the bull-creature he'd imagined on the road earlier in the day. It took every ounce of courage he could muster to get closer to the rickety building. Something on the other side squealed like a pig being dropped into a vat of boiling water. That squealing was followed by a human grunt.

Creeping over to a dirty window, Brian rubbed enough of the grime away to see Dennis Earl Gentry dancing around an altar of bones and cutting himself frantically with a buck knife. Several other people were kneeling in front of the altar and swaying rhythmically back and forth to a heavy tribal drumbeat. They chanted in unison, speaking in a low congregational monotone.

The only light in the shed came from a single bare bulb which dangled from a cord. Directly above the bare bulb was a large replica of the sun symbol made from scrap metal. An altar of animal bones had been built beneath.

Brian had heard about cults before, seen horror movies about them, and even read a book about a particular group in Jonestown, Guyana who killed themselves by drinking cyanide-laced Kool-Aid. These looked like the kind of nutcases who might do something similar.

The circle of fanatics moved counterclockwise around the fire, writhing and shaking like snake handlers over-zealous for a connection to the spiritual. Dennis Earl cut himself once more across the palm and let his blood drip over the flames where it sizzled and popped like acid. The worshipers followed suit, producing long curved knives that they used to mutilate themselves. As their chanting increased in volume, so did their enthusiasm and intensity.

9

Soon, the floor of the shed was wet with blood. Brian couldn't believe what he was seeing, and that disbelief intensified when the zealots stopped cutting themselves and started cutting each other.

The one who screamed the loudest—an overweight redneck wearing a calfskin loincloth and a crown of bones—screamed even louder and ran toward the door when the rest of the group eyed him and advanced, their knives gleaming with blood. They fell on him like hungry dogs on a piece of raw meat.

Although he wanted to run home, lock himself up in Uncle Jack's trailer, and forget all that he had seen, Brian's attention was glued to the horrific scene in the shack. Try as he might, he couldn't tear himself away. Especially when the zealots kneeling around the altar began to change.

At first Brian wasn't sure what he was seeing. The chants took on guttural tones as the kneelers began snorting like outraged animals. Hands turned into hooves. Skin turned to leather. Horns erupted from foreheads. Eyes lost all comprehension, growing large and glassy.

Before his very eyes the acolytes were turning into cattle...

Frightened and amazed, Brian stumbled away from the window, stepping on a beer can in the process. The can crunched beneath his feet, sounding like a firecracker exploding. Brian held his breath and pulled himself against the side of the shed, hoping no one had heard the noise. After a couple of minutes, he forced himself to peek through the window one last time and was surprised to see Dennis Earl Gentry peeking back at him.

Brian didn't wait to see what Dennis Earl Gentry might do to him for spying. He ran as fast as his legs would carry him back to the trailer. He thought he heard the snap of broken branches and the crackle of dead leaves once or twice, but he didn't look back to see if Dennis Earl was chasing him through the woods. His sights were set exclusively on the trailer.

He hoped that his mother would be awake and ready to give him a tongue-lashing for going out by himself at night. But she was still fast asleep on the couch. An empty bottle of wine that hadn't been there before lay beside her. That explained why she had slept through it all.

With his father's absence, Brian had taken on the mantle of the man of the house. He double and triple-checked all of the doors and windows to make sure that they were locked. The night outside was humid, and the windows were covered with condensation. Brian peered through the murky glass, searching for any sign of Dennis Earl or the other cult members. He spent no more than a couple of minutes at each window before moving to the next one, like a sentry on night patrol.

He was just about convinced that he was mistaken about what happened inside the shed when he saw a lone figure emerge from the woods. The figure was tall, lithe, cloaked in fog, and wore a leather cape. The body belonged to a man, but the head was that of a baby calf.

The calf-man lifted his head to the moon and let out a long, melancholy moan that sounded more animal than human. Soon, that dark figure was joined by several more, all of which were lowing and snorting and braying in the moonlight. The cacophony made Brian shiver uncontrollably despite the heat inside the trailer, and he quickly pulled the curtain over the window to block out the sight of the monstrosities.

The lamentations stopped immediately, and Brian

11

pulled back the curtain only to find that the woods were empty again. The calf-men were gone.

He spent the next few hours at the window, holding a vigil just in case the strange creatures returned. Eventually, the stress of the night became too much and Brian fell asleep.

When he woke up, there was a knife at his throat.

"You have no idea what you stumbled onto, boy," Dennis Earl growled, careful not to wake Janet. "But you'll find out soon enough. He's coming, you know? The signs are there for all to see. The calves are stillborn. Diseased crops bear fruit. The birds whisper amongst themselves. Even the insects make different music as they await his arrival. But that's not for the world to know. If you tell anyone what you saw, I'll kill that pretty lady over there while you sleep. Do you understand?"

To prove his point, Dennis Earl showed Brian the same knife he'd used on himself in the ritual. Brian nodded to show he understood.

"I'll be letting myself out now," Dennis Earl said. "Just remember that I've got a key to your trailer. Your Uncle Jack left it with me since I have to look in on things from time to time. I can get to you and your mother whenever I want. As long as you keep quiet, I'll never have another reason to use this key. Am I speaking your language?"

Brian nodded again, unwilling to speak.

"Good," Dennis Earl said. "I'll be seeing you around, boy."

And with that, Dennis Earl Gentry slipped out the front door. The night gobbled the man up like a delicate morsel, and soon there was no trace of him.

CHAPTER 3

E lsewhere...
The labyrinth was constructed of darkness, hatred, and black magic. At every turn, there was some grim reminder of Jeremy Martin's past waiting like a hungry dog to devour him. An empty whiskey bottle here. A one-hour motel receipt there. Around one bend there was an emaciated bank account statement that suffered from a terminal case of compulsive gambling. Hiding in another dark corner was a police report for domestic violence. Then there was the broken clock whose only purpose was to remind him of all the time he had wasted on selfish pleasures that could have been better spent with his wife and son. The reminders, however, weren't necessary.

Jeremy had done a lot of things in his lifetime that he wasn't proud of, and now it seemed that someone was using those indiscretions against him.

He didn't know how he had gotten here and couldn't recall much about the events leading up to this point. The last thing he remembered was staring down the barrel of a .45 as Jamie, the hot little blonde he'd hooked up with, gave him one last kiss goodbye.

"The Order of the Bull is going to harvest your transgressions like wheat," Jamie had said to him as she handcuffed him to the bedpost. "And to do that, we will need to keep you in a very specific place."

"I don't understand," Jeremy replied as Jamie's lithe body wavered in and out of focus. "You drugged me," he mumbled, barely noticing the sun tattoo she sported on her lower back.

"The labyrinth awaits," Jamie said as the world around Jeremy changed.

Jeremy thought about that conversation now and realized that things still didn't make sense. He was completely and thoroughly in the dark. To judge by the raucous grunts that filled the bleak hallways, however, he wasn't alone.

Although the labyrinth was dark, the walls glowed with a purple effulgence as if illuminated by black light. Strange indecipherable glyphs and sequences of raised numerals tattooed the polished stone hallways.

He cautiously touched one of the symbols and instinctively jumped back as a series of razor-tipped darts rushed past his face, missing him by inches. Inspecting the opposite wall, he noticed that the darts had been fired from a recess in the rock. No doubt, he had triggered some sort of mechanism when he ran his hands over the numbers. It was a mistake he knew he couldn't make twice.

He carefully walked the length of the gloomy hallway, looking for some way out or some other sign of a trap. He was mindful of how he placed one foot in front of the other and took extra pains to keep his hands from inadvertently touching anything.

Examining the symbols and numbers a little more closely, he noticed something that he hadn't seen before.

Although the numerals appeared to be randomly placed when you read them in the traditional method of left to right, they took on an entirely different meaning when you read them backward from right to left.

Jeremy searched the repeating cycles of digits until he finally found one that meant something to him: 29913040, or, read in reverse order and translated to a specific date, April 3, 1992. It was the day his son, Brian, had been born. Jeremy ran his fingers across the raised numerals. Immediately, a section of stone slid open at the end of the ill-lit hallway, revealing an opaque white screen.

A scene from his life flickered across the gossamer screen. Jeremy recognized St. John's Hospital. The delivery room was filled with doctors and nurses along with Janet and the fresh, pink baby that was staring at the world with wide, innocent eyes. Jeremy's heart melted at the sight of his newly born son, and he wished he had been there for such a momentous occasion. His stomach knotted up when he remembered where he'd been at the time.

The scene abruptly shifted to an after-hours club called Visions. Although he remembered exactly where he'd been while Janet gave birth to their son, it was still somewhat of a shock to see a younger version of himself stuff a crisp twenty into the G-string of a gorgeous dancer. The music in the club was quickly overshadowed by Brian's crying.

Feeling like the most wretched father in the world, he wanted the movie to stop. He jabbed angrily at one of the strange symbols on the wall that resembled a crescent moon. The short film immediately stopped playing, the opaque screen retracted into some hidden recess, and all that remained in its place was a fortune cookie. Jeremy cautiously picked up the cookie, broke it open, and read the message on the scrap of paper inside. "Guilt in all of its forms is sustenance for the gods. Escape can be found in your ability to suffer."

Jeremy didn't understand exactly what the message meant but assumed that things would become clearer in time. Of course, that was all based on the premise that he still had some time left and didn't stumble across any more booby traps.

That was also assuming that the beast roaming the dark hallways didn't find him first. Whatever was caged inside the maze with him seemed closer than ever now. It was also larger than Jeremy had first suspected. He could hear the raucous snorting of the creature, and the volume of the noises it made indicated that it was huge. It also sounded angry. Jeremy ran through the opening where he'd found the fortune cookie, hoping to hide from whatever was hot on his trail. To his dismay, the doorway didn't close once he was on the other side like it had with the poison darts.

Jeremy rapidly scanned the numbers and symbols, hoping to make some connection. His eyes raced past a familiar character and then returned to it. The symbol was a star circumscribed by a circle, or the insignia of Magellan Enterprises, who had sponsored Brian's little league baseball team. Hopeful, Jeremy touched the symbol and waited for something to happen.

A squeal of static ripped through the maze, as if someone was changing the stations on a radio. After a moment, Brian's voice came through. It was clear by the waver in his speech that he was on the verge of crying. "Why isn't Daddy here?" he asked his mother.

The radio station buzzed and then flooded with a flurry of white noise as the programming changed. Jeremy didn't need a picture of the scene to know what he was listening to. He had spent too many afternoons pressing his luck in the casinos to ignore the click of thrown dice and the subsequent cheering or sighing of the crowd.

The guttural noises of the approaching beast soon drowned out the noises of the casino...

Frantically, Jeremy raced down the hallway, looking at all the symbols and dates, trying to remember a specific time in his past when he had neglected his family. It might have been easier to pick a time when he had been the father and husband everyone wanted him to be.

At last, he found one that looked familiar.

"June 4, 1998," Jeremy said, running his fingers across the numbers. This time he heard another baby crying. Only this wasn't Brian, but another child. The infant was abruptly silenced, leaving the hallway preternaturally quiet. The abortion had cost him dearly, and it was a miracle that Janet hadn't found out about his girlfriend.

Unconcerned about the beast that was combing the hallways in hopes of devouring him, Jeremy fell to his knees and cried uncontrollably as the weight of his sins finally became too much to bear.

"You're learning," a voice said as a stone petition descended from the ceiling, sealing off part of the labyrinth. "Baal is licking his lips as we speak. He loves the taste of fear. Today, he feasts on your misery."

CHAPTER 4

Brian awoke in the recliner the next morning to the heavenly smells of frying bacon and freshly brewed coffee.

"Rise and shine," his mother said, leaving the stove long enough to give him a kiss on the forehead. Dressed smartly in a powder-gray business suit, she looked nothing at all like the woman from the night before who had been drooling slightly out of one corner of her mouth and cradling an empty wine bottle to her bosom.

"You're all dressed up. What's the occasion?" Brian asked, yawning.

"I'm job hunting today," she replied as she placed two sizzling strips of bacon on a plate.

"Today?" Brian asked, thinking about Dennis Earl's threat.

"I won't be gone all day," his mother explained. "Just promise me you'll be careful while I'm out. We still don't really know anyone around here."

"I'll be fine."

"If there are any problems maybe you could call Dennis Earl. He seemed like a nice enough guy."

It was all Brian could do not to scream in protest, yet somehow he managed to keep his temper in check. With a groan, he got out of the recliner and stretched to work all the kinks out of his muscles. He sighed as the oppressive heat of the trailer wrapped him up in a blanket of miserable warmth.

"Wish me luck," his mother said, handing him a glass of juice.

"Good luck," he said as his mother walked out the door.

After taking a sip of juice, he rifled through the newspaper his mother had left behind, searching for the comics section. He got no further than the front page.

The headline screamed, *Local Man Murdered in Ritual Slaying.*

Brian nearly spit out his juice as he recognized the man who was killed in Dennis Earl's shack the night before.

"Local officials are still baffled by the recent murder of Carson Pettigrew, age 37. Pettigrew's body was found in Reznick's Junkyard by owner Herman Reznick while doing an early morning inventory of his stock. 'Craziest thing I ever saw,' Reznick told police. 'I seen something lying underneath one of the junkers. Looked like the dogs had gotten hold of it. I went in for a closer peek, and damn, if it wasn't ol' Carson Pettigrew. I knew it was Carson because of that enormous Masonic ring he wears. Looked like somebody went to a lot of trouble to hide him there.'"

"Although police have not made an official announcement, there is speculation that this murder is actually linked to a rash of similar unsolved homicides in the area. To date, no suspects have been identified or taken in for questioning, and authorities are hesitant to officially recognize any connection. Police are baffled by any potential motive as Pettigrew, a local butcher, was generally one of the most

respected men in Crowley's Point. A devout member of The Church of Christ and the Rotary Club, Pettigrew spent his entire life in and around the October County area. He is survived by his wife, Angie, and eight-year-old son, Charlie. The Pettigrew family is offering a $10,000 reward for any leaks leading to an arrest."

It was startling to see what the murdered man had been like when he wasn't dancing around a fire and chanting the name of an ancient god. Never in a million years would Brian have suspected that Carson Pettigrew was a hard-working pillar of society, a loving husband, and a caring father. Yet, according to the article, he had been all of those things and more. It just proved that the faces people show the world sometimes aren't the ones that fit them the best.

Unwilling to sit around the trailer all day and brood about his problems, Brian decided to do something about them. He scoured the small shed behind the trailer for nearly a half hour and found only a few screws and nails, a hammer, and a screwdriver. Without other materials to work with, the stuff Brian found was useless. Fortunately, their yard, like all the others in the October County Trailer Court, had its fair share of junk, and Brian decided to search through all of it in hopes of running across something that would keep Dennis Earl out.

The grass was knee deep in most places, which obscured a lot of what was hidden in the front yard. After some careful searching, Brian found an old wooden pallet leaning against a stack of cordwood that someone had obviously been planning to use as kindling.

It took him another half hour to pry some of the boards off the pallet and drive nails through them. When he was finished, he had a couple of nasty looking spiked planks that he could place on the front doorstep or use as makeshift clubs. It wasn't a very sophisticated defense, but it would be virtually invisible at night. Brian imagined Dennis Earl creeping up to the front door and driving a two-inch nail through his foot in the process. The thought brought a smile to his face.

"You look awfully busy over there," a voice called out to him as he searched for a way to conceal the spiked plank on the upper step.

Brian whirled around to see who was speaking to him.

The man looked like a cross between Santa Claus and a Hell's Angel. Dressed in tattered jeans, black polished jack boots, and a t-shirt with a flaming skull on the front which had been stretched at impossible angles by the enormous gut underneath, the man was an imposing figure. A long white braided ponytail snaked out from beneath the man's red and blue checked bandana, running down to the center of his back. The only incongruous features were the downy white beard that looked like it was made of cotton and the kind, sparkling blue eyes that lent an air of friendliness to the man's face.

"You must be Jack's nephew," the man said. "Name's Leonard Crenshaw."

"Brian Martin. We just moved in yesterday."

"Pleased to meet you, Brian," Leonard said as he hoisted a large garbage bag over his shoulder. The contents of the bag shifted and made a familiar rattling sound that Brian had heard many times during the summer when he and his friends had scavenged for aluminum cans to make a little extra spending money.

Leonard shifted his sack from one shoulder to the other. "Jack told me your air conditioning doesn't work. I keep the thermostat in my trailer set at sixty-eight degrees. Want to

21

come in for a few minutes and grab a soda?"

Brian was just about to refuse the offer when the door to Leonard's trailer opened and the most beautiful girl Brian had ever seen stepped out.

"I've got a few minutes," he said, earning a mischievous grin from Leonard.

The girl on Leonard's front porch flashed a perfect smile at Brian and twirled a strand of strawberry blonde hair.

"Great," Leonard said. "I'll introduce you to my granddaughter, Daisy."

Brian nearly galloped up the steps. "You don't have one of those sun drawings on your front door," he remarked as he followed Leonard into the house.

Leonard's expression changed almost immediately, going from friendly and jovial to something darker. "There'll be plenty of time to talk about that," he said. "Why don't we wait until we get inside."

CHAPTER 5

Dressed in a skimpy, green bikini top, and white cotton shorts, Daisy had the kind of figure that lassoed drooling adolescent boys and hauled them into puberty. Flaming red hair and emerald eyes gave her a certain exotic look that made her seem much more experienced than her eighteen years would suggest. Brian was immediately smitten. His eyes stayed locked on Daisy for little more than a few seconds, however, before he noticed the rest of the room.

In lieu of furniture, beer cans had been shaped, welded, and hammered into a coffee table that sat in the center of the room. Matching beer-can sofa tables flanked the ratty loveseat and the similarly-built entertainment center that looked like a shrine to the great god, Michelob. Budweiser, Coors, and Colt .45 remains positioned atop each of the sofa tables bore uncanny resemblances to Hank Williams Jr and Richard Petty. Aluminum animals frolicked, jumped, and sprinted along one wall, frozen in various states of still life. Leonard had even crafted an imitation trophy deer head made of cans which peered down at them with coke-bottle eyes from the wall opposite the front door. The centerpiece of the room, however, was an odd facsimile of the Nativity done up in Milwaukee's Best and Natural Lite. In a gesture of decency, the baby Jesus had been constructed from non-alcoholic beer cans.

"Wow," Brian said. It was the only word that seemed appropriate.

"It's just a little hobby of mine," Leonard chuckled. Leonard's chuckling was cut short by Daisy's elbow to his gut, signaling the need for an introduction. "Oh, right," he said. "I almost forgot. Brian, this is my granddaughter, Daisy. Daisy, this is Brian Martin. He's Jack's nephew. He just moved in next door."

"Nice to meet you," Brian said.

"You too," Daisy said, blushing slightly as she turned away to hide her smile. As she did so, Brian couldn't help noticing the brand on her lower back that resembled a blazing sun.

Brian looked to Leonard for an explanation, remembering the way he'd reacted initially when the subject came up. "I guess you want to know about the sun symbol," Leonard said. "You just moved in, so I feel I owe it to your Uncle Jack to tell you everything you need to know."

"I was curious about the symbol," Brian admitted. "I saw a mark just like that one on Dennis Earl Gentry's shoulder."

"Dennis Earl sure didn't waste any time with you," Leonard said as he sat down to his breakfast. "That can't be a good sign."

"I saw him last night. Him and a bunch of others."

Leonard and Daisy exchanged a nervous glance. "The group you saw call themselves The Order of the Bull. They're the ones with those sun symbols painted on their front doors. They're a dangerous bunch to be sure. I'd steer clear of them if I were you."

24

"I've got one of those symbols on my door," Brian realized. "Are you saying that Uncle Jack was a member of that group?"

Leonard shook his head. "He painted that on the door when he first moved here. He hoped that it would be a measure of protection if The Order believed that he respected them and what they believed. It's kind of like wearing the right color bandana on gang turf."

"So how did you get that mark?" Brian asked Daisy.

Daisy looked like she'd been slapped. "I don't like to talk about it," she said. "Let's just say it wasn't by choice."

"Sorry I asked," Brian said. "What do these people believe?"

Leonard took a big bite of eggs and a swig of coffee before answering. "Basically, they believe that every piece of ground is ruled by a territorial god. This god can bring about prosperity or ruin. They hope to ensure their own prosperity by worshiping the Baalim that lords over the ground that the trailer park is built on. In mythology, Baal is usually depicted as a bull. The sun symbol represents fertility and the prosperity that Baal gives to his followers."

"This is crazy," Brian said. "But it kinda makes sense."

"What, exactly, did you see, boy?" Leonard asked, eyes narrowing. "Don't leave out one little detail."

Brian recounted the scene in as much detail as he could remember. When he was done, he noticed that the color had drained out of Leonard's features.

"They may have actually done it," Leonard said, shaking his head. "They may have actually gotten Baal's attention with that little stunt."

"You believe in this stuff?" Brian asked, surprised. "You think those people really changed into cattle because they murdered Pettigrew?"

25

"I've seen a lot of things around here that have made me keep an open mind."

"The only thing that will make me believe is proof, and tonight, I'm going to catch Dennis Earl on video."

Daisy and Leonard exchanged puzzled glances.

"I would leave him alone if I were you," Leonard advised. "You're getting in over your head. Dennis Earl's a real rattlesnake."

"I'm all my mother has," Brian explained. "I can't beat him in a fight, so I need to outsmart him."

"These people are bad news," Daisy reiterated.

Leonard sighed. "Dennis Earl will put you in the ground, boy."

"Nothing you say is going to change my mind," Brian replied.

"I'll go with you then," Daisy said. "You don't know your way around. It would be suicide without me."

"I don't know if that's such a good idea," Leonard said.

"He'll get caught if I'm not there to help him," Daisy said. "You know I can take care of myself."

Leonard sighed. "I don't like it, but I guess I owe it to Jack to help out. He's done a lot for me in the past. I promised him I would tend to his family as best I could."

"I can take care of myself," Brian argued.

"I'm coming whether you like it or not," Daisy said. "If you try to sneak out without me, I'll just follow you. Face it, you're stuck with me tonight."

Brian sighed, thinking to himself that it might not be so bad. Alone in the dark woods with a beautiful girl. Seemed like a no-brainer. "Okay," he consented.

"I'll see you at midnight," Daisy said.

Brian walked away with a faint smile playing on his lips and a light bounce in his step. It was almost as if he had forgotten that he was going to secure evidence on a cult that had no qualms about murdering in cold blood.

Daisy waited until Brian had gone back to his trailer before looking at Leonard. "I just hope The Sect of the Calf doesn't mess things up," she said.

"Hush, girl," Leonard barked. "We're not going to think that way."

CHAPTER 6

lsewhere...

The key to opening more doors and finding the way out of the maze involved finding more dates that he recognized. Jeremy found another one after five minutes of searching. It was the day he and Janet got married. He rubbed the glowing numerals and wasn't surprised when another door opened to reveal a fully stocked wet bar that looked every bit like the one he'd patronized on his wedding night after walking out on Janet. Surprisingly enough, someone had poured a sea breeze for him, and he knew that he was supposed to take a drink. The only thing missing was a Lewis Carroll-type sign that read 'Drink Me.'

He sipped the drink and instantly found himself adrift on an ocean of turbulent memories. He saw Janet crying on the cheap motel bed. She was still wearing her wedding dress. A large red splotch in the shape of a hand marked her face. Jeremy couldn't even remember what had started the argument, but he remembered slapping her. Janet spent the night alone, and he spent the majority of the evening getting wasted in a bar.

He felt sick. He was starting to see first-hand what type of person he really was, and he didn't like it at all.

He liked it even less when the stone petition lifted, and the minotaur eyed him from the shadows. The beast was black, covered in a pelt of coarse hair resembling midnight, and crowned with a set of wicked horns that were wet with fresh blood.

Jeremy ran blindly and heard the smack of hooves on stone not too far behind him. The noises of pursuit stopped, however, once he rounded a corner and found himself standing in what could have passed for a carbon copy of his living room. There was no trace of the minotaur. It was as if he had stepped from one world into another.

The only sounds he could hear now were those of Janet and Brian arguing upstairs. They were familiar sounds, sounds that made his heart ache just a little bit. It had been a while since he'd heard anything like it.

"I hate him. I don't care what you say!" Brian screamed. "How could he leave us?"

Jeremy's heart sank.

"Brian, he's still your father," Janet reminded him.

"I don't have a father. I never have."

Jeremy felt the knife in his chest twist, and he grimaced at the pain. A single tear rolled down his cheek. How had things gotten to this point?

He took the stairs two at a time, expecting to find Janet and Brian. What he found instead was another dark hallway. Instead of symbols and numbers, the walls up here were covered in Polaroids, detailing the various exploits he'd participated in with women who weren't his wife. A tortured groan escaped his lips when he saw the monster the camera had photographed and realized that the monster wore his face.

"Stop it," he cried out to anyone who might have been listening. "I'm a bad husband and father. I'm a miserable excuse for a human being. You've made your point. What do you want from me?"

From somewhere close by the minotaur howled in reply.

Frustrated, Jeremy began ripping the Polaroids off the walls and tearing them into little pieces. A mirror glared back at him from the newly vacated place on the labyrinth wall. Jeremy screamed when he saw a minotaur staring back at him and realized the implications. He had truly become a monster. Or maybe he'd been one all along.

He smashed the mirror with his fist and smiled when the million fragmented bits of polished glass reflected the face he recognized. Jeremy screamed, this time out of rage and an impending sense of guilt. The sound that ripped from his lungs, however, wasn't human anymore. It was the sound of an angry bull that has been prodded one too many times by the matador.

CHAPTER 7

Brian reluctantly walked toward the oven-like purgatory of his trailer, his mind full of random thoughts. He had made it nearly halfway back to the trailer when he saw the bleached bull skull sitting on the top step. He looked around cautiously, wondering who had placed the skull there and why.

Skewered on one of the horns was a scrap of paper. "The Sect of the Calf will destroy the maze that Baal has built."

Brian reread the note twice, more confused now than ever.

Brian suddenly detected movement off to his right and turned to see the knee-high grass billowing back and forth. Someone was running away. Acting on instinct, he raced after the trail of moving branches and trampled leaves.

As Brian closed the gap, he could make out a few details about the person ahead of him. The runner was big and quick, moving through the underbrush with the speed and brute force of a linebacker. A halo of flies circled an oversized, misshapen head. In the runner's wake was a stench that was a gagging combination of rotting garbage and barnyard slop.

Yet it was only when the runner passed through a shaft of light that Brian saw the horns...

Brian ran as fast as he could and emerged from the forest just in time to see the creature enter a dingy white cinderblock building that had the faded word 'slaughterhouse' painted on the side. He hesitated at this point, unsure if he should go in by himself or not. He hadn't brought a weapon of any kind or even a flashlight.

The calf-faced creature poked its head out long enough to fix Brian with a glassy-eyed stare. Fearfully, Brian followed after him.

He was surprised to find the room full of activity once he stepped inside. Only the outlines of the creatures were visible in the dark, but Brian could discern enough about them to note horns and hooves.

Although it had been years since the slaughterhouse had contained livestock, something lowed at him from the shadows like a sick calf. The lowing sound turned into the sound of a child laughing.

The horned creatures bowed at the sound and rubbed their horns on the cement in some unexplained gesture of worship. The thing masquerading as an ailing calf made a garbled mooing sound from the shadows. The sound was hideous and made Brian want to run and hide. Yet, he realized the sound for what it was: pure and unadulterated pleasure.

The sick calf was happy about something.

The light that filtered in through the briefly opened door showed a glimpse of the sick calf, and that was enough to give Brian nightmares for the rest of his life. The animal was albino and covered in flies. Its eyes had milky cataracts, and its legs were horribly deformed. A black tongue coated with a white fuzz lolled out of one side of its mouth, oblivious to the tiny bugs that crawled over it. "What do you want from me?" Brian asked. The creatures snorted and bellowed and went from two legs to all fours.

The sick calf bleated and cried and turned its blind eyes toward Brian. "We need your help," it said simply. "The Order of the Bull must be stopped. Baal must not be raised. The Order doesn't understand the kind of power they're dealing with. We were like them once and have paid for our mistakes. The one they serve doesn't honor loyalty. Instead, it revels in pain and misery."

No elaborations were given, and soon the creatures didn't even seem to notice that Brian was there anymore. Brian wasn't sure what these creatures thought he could do, and they didn't seem to want to give him any additional information. He walked out of the slaughterhouse feeling confused, scared, and a little angry.

Wanting only to get away from that horrid place, Brian sprinted back to the trailer, his mind racing out of control, wondering what he could say or do to convince his mother to leave.

"We've gotta get out of here," he panted as he burst through the door. His mother was just taking off her suit jacket, obviously done with her interviews for the day.

"What's wrong?" she asked. "Are you okay?"

"We need to leave now."

"Brian, did somebody hurt you?" Janet persisted.

Brian composed himself and took a second to catch his breath, making a last-minute decision to leave out the part about The Sect of the Calf. "Mom, I need you to listen to me. What I say is going to sound crazy, but it's true."

Janet Martin stared at her son. The look on her face wasn't a look of all-out worry, but it was getting there.

"What do you need to tell me?" she asked.

Brian led his mother over to the plaid, beer-stained couch and motioned for her to sit. "There are a lot of things going on here that you don't know about. These aren't nice people we're living with. They're murderers. Or at least some of them are. I saw them last night."

"Murderers?" Janet said with an edge of doubt in her voice.

"Everyone who has one of those sun symbols painted on the door belongs to a cult called The Order of the Bull. They worship Baal. I saw them sacrifice a man last night. Dennis Earl Gentry is a member of that cult. He's threatened to kill you if I tell anyone what I saw. That's why we have to leave right away."

Janet didn't say anything for a moment. It was clear that Brian's story had taken her by surprise, and her face was a battleground for warring emotions. She wanted to believe her son, but she also found the story incredible.

"Let me get this straight," she said. "Everyone here is a member of a murderous cult that worships Baal?"

"The Order of the Bull," Brian said. "That's what they call themselves."

"You said you saw them last night. You were supposed to be here with me. Did you sneak out?"

"I heard some noise and went to check it out. You were asleep, and I didn't want to wake you."

Janet nodded. "You said anyone who has those symbols on the door is a cult member. We have a symbol like that on our door."

"Uncle Jack did that," Brian explained.

"So, Uncle Jack's a cult member now?"

Brian shrugged his shoulders. This wasn't going like he had hoped it would. "They murdered a man, mom. I wouldn't make something like that up."

Janet chewed on that thought for a moment. "If that's the case then I should call the police."

"No, don't you understand? You can't do that!" Brian screamed. "Dennis Earl warned me about what he would do to you."

"All right, I've had just about enough of this," Janet said, her temper flaring. "I'm calling Jack."

Brian hadn't expected this. If anyone might know what was really going on here, it *would* be Uncle Jack. Janet used the speakerphone option on her cell phone and dialed Jack's number. Jack Martin picked up after a couple of rings. In this sea of hellish uncertainty, his deep, somber voice was a steady anchor. Brian felt better just hearing him.

"Jack, it's Janet. I'm sorry to bother you but I've got a quick question."

"No problem, Janet. I hope everything's going okay for you and Brian. I'm sorry I haven't been able to help out more."

"You've done more than enough," Janet said. "You've let us live in your home when we had no home of our own. It's a chance to start fresh after everything that happened with Jeremy. He walked out and left us with nothing."

"Don't think anything about it," Jack said. "I had already planned to be gone on business for a few weeks. My place was empty. No reason you and Brian shouldn't use it as a place to regroup while you figured out your next move."

"It's much appreciated. But, we've got a slight problem here. Do you know anything about a group of people calling themselves The Order of the Bull? Brian claims that they are some sort of murdering cult that lives here in the trailer park."

Jack didn't say anything for a few seconds. It was clear the nature of the call had taken him aback. "There's no cult there that I know of," he said at last.

Janet looked at Brian with a discerning look of satisfaction. "What about Dennis Earl Gentry?"

"He's kind of a rough character, but I don't know that he's ever murdered anybody."

"Okay, Jack. I'm sorry to bother you. I just wanted to clear things up. Brian's a little upset."

"Brian's going through a rough time right now," Jack said. "Go easy on him. I'm sure he didn't mean any harm. Kids act out sometimes when they need a little extra attention."

"He's lying," Brian said through clenched teeth. "He knows what's happening here. Ask him about the sun symbols—"

"Enough," Janet said.

"But—" Brian persisted.

"I'll talk to you later, Jack," Janet said, ending the call. "And thanks again."

"Don't mention it, Janet. Oh, and one more thing. I'm sorry about my brother. He never deserved you."

"Thank you," Janet said before hanging up the phone. "I mean that."

"He's lying, mom," Brian said once it was clear she was off the call. "He's one of them."

"I know that you don't want to be here. Neither do I. But making up a story like that is not going to magically make a house appear for us somewhere else. This is where we're living until I can do better."

"Mom, I swear to you that I'm telling the truth."

"I don't want to hear another word about Uncle Jack, murder, or this cult. I think you're just hoping that I'll agree

36

to pack up and leave. It's not that simple. We don't have any other place to go."

"But Mom—"

"Go to your room," Janet said. "I will not tolerate being lied to."

Brian did as he was told and wondered if his mother would ever truly understand how difficult she made things sometimes.

Chapter 8

Elsewhere...

The labyrinth seemed to be a place of metaphor and madness, and Jeremy tried to embrace that concept, imagining his life as a withered, diseased tree standing against a sky the color of burnished gunmetal. Memories, like brittle leaves, were scattered about the dead landscape. He would have enjoyed nothing more than to rake all those leaves into a pile and set fire to them, hoping to start fresh in the spring. Yet he knew that wasn't the way nature worked. You didn't get a second chance to live your life. The mistakes you made were as immutable and permanent as scars. Jeremy felt like he had been mutilated beyond recognition.

He remembered the fortune cookie message that said, "Escape can be found in your ability to suffer," and wondered why he hadn't found his way out of this maze yet. He had suffered tremendously, both physically and mentally. Of course, his version of suffering and his captor's were probably very different.

Although the roster of people who hated him looked like a grocery list, there were only a few with the means and capabilities of pulling off something this elaborate. That list could be narrowed down even further when you considered the ones who dabbled in magicks and conjuring.

Jeremy had experimented enough with the black arts in his time to know that speaking someone's name gave them power, so he wasn't about to do anything that foolish here in his captor's domain. Still, that didn't mean he couldn't picture the man's face in his mind. It was a familiar face. A face he had once trusted and even loved before he lost the capacity for such a thing.

The face that greeted him at the end of the labyrinth wasn't that sort of face. Rather, it was the face of a bull.

"Escape can be found in your ability to suffer," Jeremy repeated in his mind as he prepared to fight what could be the last battle of his life.

The minotaur eyed him carefully, and Jeremy knew that he was no better than this horrid creature. The pull of his old self tugged hard at his heart, and Jeremy knew that there was no other choice but to embrace the beast he had become. His transformation began suddenly.

He could feel the blood coursing down his cheeks as the horns poked through first skull and then skin. His jaws stretched and his feet hardened into hooves. His rib cage expanded until it felt like his chest would explode, spilling all of his vitals onto the labyrinth floor. His skin sloughed off, and the tender dermis beneath toughened, thickened, and grew a heavy coating of coarse black hair. Yet, despite all of the physiological changes, he felt alive and powerful and every bit the sort of man who could walk away from an old life and transform himself into a new creature.

The life depicted on opaque screens and in the subtle hints of strategically placed items in the maze wasn't the life he wanted for himself anymore. He wanted his wife and son back. He wanted his family back. But he knew the only way to achieve that was to kill his opponent and all of the base desires his opponent represented.

The roar Jeremy let loose was the culmination of frustration, rage, and determination. The roar he received in reply was one of hatred and of power. Jeremy shuddered, and then he swallowed his fear.

He charged at his opponent, arms held out in front of him like battering rams. His minotaur captor rushed at him with equal fervor, horns lowered like lances in a joust. The two of them clashed with a loud smack, and it took Jeremy a moment to realize that he had broken one of the minotaur's horns. The blood, however, was what alerted him to the fact that he had sustained some damage in the process.

The horn jutted from his side, and he pulled it out gently. Blood jettisoned from the wound, wetting the walls of the labyrinth in a fine pink mist. There wasn't time to contemplate the severity of his wounds, however. Already his opponent was on his feet and charging again, his eyes glowing with a smoldering heat that was reminiscent of twin suns on the verge of supernova.

Jeremy waited until the last possible minute, then dropped to his knees. He landed a quick punch to the minotaur's midsection that knocked the air from his lungs. He grabbed the broken piece of horn to use as a weapon, but he didn't get the chance to use it. Despite its injuries, the minotaur was quick enough to constrict Jeremy's neck with one of its powerful arms, successfully cutting off the flow of oxygen.

Jeremy floundered and struggled to free himself from the stranglehold. He'd managed to hold onto the minotaur's broken horn and jabbed blindly over his shoulder with the makeshift dagger. The minotaur howled in pain and flailed, pushing him away. Jeremy turned and saw that the horn protruding from the minotaur's right eye.

With both of them bleeding now, the levels of danger, fear, and adrenaline were elevated.

Jeremy broadsided his attacker, knocking him to the floor. Quickly, he rammed his thumb into the bloodied ocular socket and pushed as hard as he could. Sent into a frenzy by the excruciating pain, the minotaur bucked and successfully threw Jeremy off. But Jeremy was determined. He was back on top of the minotaur before the creature could gain his footing, and he tore the beast's neck open. Hot fluids spurted in wide, scarlet arcs, covering Jeremy's face and chest. He opened his mouth to taste the victory and closed his eyes to block out the sight of what he'd done. If he ever got back to reality, he hoped to leave the monster inside him behind and embrace the man.

It was only when he opened his eyes that he realized the spell was broken. Gone were all traces of the labyrinth, the minotaur, and the bad memories. All that remained was the dingy roach-infested excesses of the motel where he and Jamie had spent the night. The keys to the handcuffs were lying on the nightstand. Apparently, Jamie hadn't thought it likely that he would survive the maze.

After freeing himself and walking out into the sun he wondered where his family might be and realized that there was only one sure bet. He had taken every bit of money and left them with nothing. They would have had to rely on someone in the family to take them in or give them a place to stay.

The truck's engine roared to life on the first try, and Jeremy pointed it in the direction of October County. He just prayed that his family would give him a chance to make restitution for all the things he had done wrong.

Chapter 9

At a little before midnight, Brian stepped into darkness, armed with his video recorder and one of the spiked planks he'd made. He was surprised to see an oppressive layer of fog had crept in, carried on currents of cool night air.

Raising the camcorder to his eye, Brian peered through the lens and realized right away that it was going to be difficult to get any decent footage in these kinds of conditions.

Heat lightning streaked through the heavens like the vapor trails of falling angels. Somewhere in the distance, cattle lowed. The clamor was enough to raise the hair on his arms and neck. Shivering in fear, he pulled his jacket tightly around him although there was nothing the slick nylon material could do to combat the chill of trepidation.

On his way across the overgrown front yard, Brian peeped through the living room window to make sure his mother was still sleeping. Her gentle snores convinced him she was dreaming fitfully.

Satisfied, he was about to look for Daisy when a hand gripped his shoulder, nearly ripping a scream from his lungs that would wake the dead.

"Jeez," Brian hissed, raising the spiked plank in defense. He lowered the weapon once he saw who it was.

"You're awful jumpy," Daisy laughed. "Clubbing a girl went out of fashion with the cavemen, you know?"

"Sorry," Brian said. "I was just getting ready to look for you."

"Well look no further," Daisy said, her tone a little more playful than it had been earlier in the day. Although Brian wasn't certain of anything, it seemed like there was a marked change in Daisy. Before, she had seemed the shy, bashful type. Now, she had an edge to her that made her even more beautiful and alluring.

"Are you sure you still want to do this?" he asked.

"I wouldn't miss this for the world," she said. "Did you bring the camera?"

Brian held it up to show her.

"I know a shortcut," she said. "Try to keep up."

The path that snaked through the woods wasn't so much a path as it was a swath made by persistent feet. Briars and thorns ripped at their skin, drawing thin lines of blood. Fallen trees and broken limbs blocked the path in some places, forcing them to go even deeper into the underbrush. Thick white smoke trailed through the forest, mingling with the fog and haze. Up ahead, just past the edge of the forest where the land had been cleared away for more trailers, Brian could see what looked to be a large bonfire.

Rednecks danced around the altar of bones. Some of the zealots wore crowns made of bull horns. Others were clothed in the pelts of young calves. Some had rings in their noses, while others had been bridled and saddled. Brian watched in horror as two men took turns pressing a white hot brand to their chests, leaving the now-familiar sun imprint on their sizzling skin.

Dennis Earl Gentry was nowhere to be found.

"They're having church," Daisy explained. "This is their form of worship."

Brian nodded, pretending to understand while his finger remained on the 'record' button. Daisy pressed close to him and held his hand as they crept closer and closer to the ceremony. The lowing of cattle was louder now, although there seemed to be no livestock nearby. That sound was quickly overshadowed by the roar of a powerful engine.

Brian watched in confusion as Dennis Earl's red, white, and blue tow truck pulled into the clearing, hauling something large and indiscernible. "We've got to get closer," he said. "I've zoomed in as much as the camera will allow."

Daisy crept forward and pulled Brian with her. When he saw what was on the back of the tow truck, he pulled away.

"What is this?" he asked as the zealots around the altar of bones helped take an enormous metallic bull made of beer cans down from its pedestal atop the tow truck. One by one, the acolytes of Baal knelt before the idol and pledged their allegiance in the form of a kiss. Brian barely had time to register this fact before he heard a branch snap somewhere behind him. He turned just in time to see Leonard rushing at him with a branding iron.

CHAPTER 10

Brian opened his eyes, trying to remember what had happened to him. His temple throbbed, and something sticky covered the side of his face. He groaned in pain and looked around at the zealots enraptured by the prospect of meeting their god. A pile of bleached animal bones had been heaped and shaped into a low-lying mound upon which a throne of bones rested. Atop the throne was Leonard, looking like a barbarian king, wearing a crown made of barbed wire, and a set of viciously curved horns.

Seeing Leonard was the only trigger Brian needed for the memories of Daisy's betrayal to come flooding back.

He frantically tried to sit up only to realize that he had been hog tied with something that felt stronger than rope. Baling wire perhaps. Enraged, he fought against his restraints which only made the bonds tighter, cutting off the circulation in his hands.

He tried to scream out in frustration and anger, but the gag in his mouth prevented it. Leonard saw him struggling and stepped off his throne. Even with the noise made by the drums and the chanting, Brian could still hear the

45

crunch of breaking bone underneath Leonard's feet.

"He's coming," the cultists chanted as Leonard approached.

Leonard didn't say anything to Brian but instead made a circular, ceremonial motion with his hands that set the group into a frenzy of flailing limbs and gibbering tongues. One by one, the zealots knelt before the massive aluminum idol and kissed the hooves in a gesture of reverence and obedience. Leonard grabbed the wire that had been used to tie Brian up and hauled him to his feet.

Brian hadn't noticed it at first, but the idol was equipped with two curving scimitar blades that served as horns. A pulley system and a series of ropes had been set up directly above the idol. Leonard dragged Brian over to the tree where the pulleys had been installed and snapped him in using a carabiner.

"Our god won't show without blood," Leonard explained, his eyes gleaming fanatically in the night. "But he'll be here soon enough. You'll see to that."

Using his weight as a counterbalance, Leonard hoisted Brian into the air. He had no doubt that he was about to be sacrificed to Baal and impaled on one of those wicked looking blades.

Daisy separated from the group and gave Brian a quick kiss on the cheek as he was lifted into the air. She pulled the gag away and smiled as he screamed.

"You lied to me," he yelled.

"Baal is honored by lies," she said, turning around to show the sun symbol on her back.

Adding insult to injury was Dennis Earl who sidled up beside her and put his arm around her waist. He kissed Daisy long and hard, letting his tongue frolic inside her mouth. Once they were finished, he offered her a knife.

"Shall we begin, darlin?" he asked.

Daisy responded by cutting him long and deep across the midriff, drawing a thin trickle of blood.

"Kill him," Dennis Earl shouted to Leonard.

Leonard used all of his weight to pull on the rope as Brian shot into the air. He screamed one last time as he was positioned over the sharp horns of the brazen bull.

"He's here," the cultists whispered reverently. *"He's finally here."*

Brian craned his neck, expecting to see the minotaur made flesh. Nothing, however, could have prepared him for what he actually saw. The man before him was well over six feet tall and sported overalls and a salt-and-pepper beard that hung down mid-torso. He wore a John Deere cap and looked to have a jaw full of tobacco. He spit off to the side once before tucking his chew tighter into his cheek and speaking in a low, sinister voice.

"Hello Brian," Uncle Jack said as he stood there holding a body in his arms. "Isn't this a pleasant surprise?"

All Brian could do was scream when he realized that the unconscious woman in Uncle Jack's clutches was his mother.

CHAPTER 11

O nce he found the trailer court, Jeremy didn't have to look hard to find Janet and Brian. Smoke from the bonfire curled high into the sky, marking the site as effectively as a neon sign.

It took a few seconds for Jeremy to recognize that the boy dangling precariously above the sacrificial bull was Brian and the unconscious woman in Jack's arms was Janet.

"I should have known you were behind all of this, Jack," Jeremy said as he stepped out of his truck.

Jack laughed. "Who else do you think set you up with that little floozy? I know your weakness, little brother. Baal thrives on despair, and your family was a veritable wellspring."

"You planned my family's destruction," Jeremy roared.

Jack shook his head. "You planned that yourself, bro. You sowed the seeds of your family's discontent. I just reaped the harvest."

"I'm going to kill you."

"The smartest thing you could do right now is to walk away from this and never look back," Jack said. "The transmogrification is almost complete, and Baal will be raised. Trust me when I say that you don't want to be here when that happens."

Jeremy pulled out a .357 Magnum. "The smartest thing you can do is to shut up and get Brian out of that harness. I don't care which god you serve, all the praying in the world won't protect you from a bullet to the head."

The acolytes stopped their dancing and worship at the sight of the gun.

"You don't understand anything," Jack said. "But you soon will. Baal will show himself tonight, and he will clothe himself in my skin."

The changes in Jack were like nothing Jeremy had ever seen, and he had a difficult time believing that this was the same brother he used to play baseball with in the front yard. Instead of a single set of horns, three rows of black pointed bone sprouted from his forehead. Hooves were forsaken in lieu of hands that ended in claws. Teeth normally designed for chewing cud and grazing sharpened and elongated, giving Jack the look of a natural born predator.

The gun felt like little more than a toy in Jeremy's hand.

The changes in Jack prompted the changes in everyone else. Men walking on two legs reverted to all fours. Flesh became hide. Eyes widened and darkened. Bones stretched, muscles expanded. Voices deepened and lost the ability of speech.

Much to Jeremy's surprise, Jack's normally confident eyes were suddenly filled with fear.

Jeremy turned around and was shocked to see what looked like a cross between men and calves standing behind him. Their torsos were scarred. Their bodies were pierced. Sun brands marked their flesh. They stood upright on legs that ended in hooves. The fact that they had the faces of baby cattle did nothing to hide the

49

righteous anger that galvanized their every expression.

"The time has come," one of them bleated. "This is going to end tonight."

"Indeed," Jack replied, like a general surveying the site of an upcoming battle.

When both sides rushed at each other, Jeremy thought he was a dead man for sure. The clash and crackle of horns locking and breaking off was thunderous. The cattle were no longer lowing. They were making long, agonizing noises that might well have been music to Baal's ears.

Jeremy scrambled up the flank of the massive aluminum bull. He couldn't help noticing the rust-colored stains on the bull's horns. This idol had been appeased before.

Carefully, Jeremy pulled on the wire that held Brian in the air and flicked his Buck knife open.

Brian trembled in the makeshift harness. "Don't let me fall!"

"I won't let anything happen to you," Jeremy said as he used the blade to saw through the thin wire. The moment he felt the restraint snap, he threw his weight backward, pulling Brian with him. Brian hit the back of the bull with a loud clang.

For a moment it was touch and go as Brian scrabbled to maintain a grip on the slick beast. The treads of his sneakers finally found traction and he was able to sit up with his father's help. Jeremy hugged his son close to him, inhaling the familiar scent of sweat masked by Calvin Klein cologne. Tears streamed down his face as he realized just how much of his life he had thrown away.

"What are you doing here?" Brian asked. "I never thought I'd see you again."

"I've done a lot of things I'm ashamed of," Jeremy said. "I've neglected you and your mom. But this isn't the right time or place for apologies. Let's just say that I'm a new man now and leave it at that. We can sort the rest out once we're sure we're going to get out of this alive."

Brian nodded, his face a strange mixture of indecision and irritation. "Let's go get Mom," he said as the howling around them reached new heights. The fight had moved into the woods where shadows abounded, making it difficult to see what exactly was going on.

Jeremy helped Brian to the ground and then scurried down the side of the bull. They both froze when they saw the creature Jack had transformed into leaning against the tow truck. He cradled Janet like a baby in his arms.

"Looking for something," he snorted, licking the side of her face with his overlong cow's tongue. "She's good and drugged up just like you like 'em. I made sure of that."

"Put her down and fight me like a man," Jeremy said.

Jack guffawed as he tossed Janet to the ground like an unwanted toy. "Well, the only problem with that is that I'm not a man anymore."

"Fight me," Jeremy growled.

Jack nodded in resignation, bowed once, and went down on all fours. The cloud of flies swarming around him followed his every movement like a shifting skin. "Baal will be glorified through the spilling of your blood," he said.

Jeremy clutched the knife tightly in one hand and the pistol in the other. He knew his weapons would probably have little effect on the creature that his brother had become. But he wasn't going to go down without a fight. "Take care of your mother," he said quietly to Brian as he prepared to die.

All Jeremy saw in front of him was the beast from the labyrinth, and the sight of such a creature was enough to bring back the memories of the monster he used to be.

51

That beast, he knew, was the only rival that was capable of defeating Jack. Although he wanted to embrace the new man he had become and cast away all of the old habits and desires, he knew he couldn't do so just yet. He needed all of the hatred and lust and guilt.

As strange ritual magics swirled in the air, Jeremy realized that he could tap into that energy just as the cult members had. He allowed himself to regress to what he had been inside the dream-like haze of the labyrinth. Whatever sort of spell they had cast still had its hooks in him, and he didn't resist the urge to transform. He felt himself begin to change, and he hated himself more than he ever had while trolling the depths of a bottle or scouring the city streets for female companionship. The labyrinth and everything that had happened there had all been stepping stones leading up to this point. The legacy of who he used to be devoured him and spat him back out in disgust.

Like an ill-fitting suit of skin, the minotaur that used to be Jeremy cast off every nuance of humanity and studied its adversary with eyes that looked like drowning pools filled with rage and disgust.

The beastly brothers eyed each other, pawed at the dirt, and exhaled swirling clouds of smoke as they lowered their heads to display the impressive threat of razor-tipped horns. Without warning, both of them charged. The collision of skulls made a crackling noise like dead trees being snapped in the hands of giants.

Brian looked over his shoulder once as he ran toward his mother and saw his father change into something alien.

"Mom, wake up," he said, lightly slapping his mother's cheeks. Janet's eyes fluttered like insect wings, and she exhaled softly.

The bulls charged at each other again behind them.

Brian watched his father open his jaws and take a chunk of flesh out of Jack's flank. He watched Jack rear up and kick his father in the face with a hoof, smacking his father's lips and shattering some of his teeth.

"Mom, come on," he said with a little more urgency. But Janet didn't move. Whatever drug Jack had given her had been incredibly potent.

Brian glanced around nervously, wondering how much time he had left before the fight came to them. He got his answer when he saw something that bore a striking resemblance to Dennis Earl Gentry stride out of the dark woods, looking exactly as he had on that first day. His body was wiry, covered in scars and sweat, and topped by a bull's head.

"I've been meaning to pay your mother a visit," he said as he walked confidently toward them, clenching and unclenching his fists. "I've liked her from the moment I first laid eyes on her."

Brian looked for something to use as a weapon but didn't see anything useful. "Stay away from us," he said, standing up to guard his mother.

Dennis Earl shook his head and made an expression that might have been a smile. It was a horrid gesture that looked frightfully out of place on an otherwise bovine face.

The look changed to one of surprise when the aluminum idol turned its head to stare back at him.

CHAPTER 12

The gleaming idol moved sluggishly at first as if shaking off the last vestiges of death. It looked at Brian without a single trace of emotion, like a giant studying a tiny scuttling ant. The blank face shimmered and changed once it swiveled to study Dennis Earl. The disinterest was immediately transformed into a mixture of anger and hatred.

Dennis Earl went down to all fours and then knelt before Baal, his horns tracing small lines in the dirt as he prayed in a bovine tongue.

The aluminum bull lowered its horns and rushed at the minotaur, goring him and flinging him into the air. Dennis Earl howled as his skewered body sailed into a tree and slid down the trunk, leaving a messy smear of blood on the bark.

"I don't understand," he gasped. He tried to get to his feet only to collapse onto the messy carpet of wet grass and leaves.

"Baal delights in agony," Jack said as he temporarily turned his attention away from his transformed brother and focused on the god he had been so fervently trying to

54

raise. "I can't believe he's finally here."

Jeremy saw his opportunity and charged, planting his unbroken horn into Jack's leathery side. Jack screamed out in pain and surprise, and Baal reared up on his hind legs, snorting and bellowing. The aluminum facade that the god wore began to fragment like poorly tempered mirrored glass. Cracks ran in every direction like spider webs, and bits of aluminum flaked away, showing something much stranger beneath.

The image of a bull was merely a facade to hide the true face of the god, and here in an orchard where pain and lamentations grew ripe like fruit on the vine, Baal was strong enough to manifest. Baal turned toward the two minotaurs, thought for a moment, and rushed at Jack. With each step, bits of the metal that helped keep its form fell away. The human confines that held the god would be cast off within minutes, and then, it would be impossible to say what form it would take.

Upon seeing his god stride confidently into this life with rage and a regal hatred of natural order, Jack spoke a quick prayer and knelt as Dennis Earl had done, wishing for a slow death so that Baal might savor his agony. The bull-god rammed him at full speed, shattering every bone in his body.

Jeremy watched Baal with caution and turned his bovine head toward Brian and Janet. "Go while I'm stalling this thing," he said. "If this doesn't show you how sorry I am then nothing will. I love you both."

"No," Brian screamed as Jeremy rushed at the bull-god with his head down like a battering ram. A huge chunk of aluminum sloughed off, revealing more of the true essence of Baal, leaving a gaping black hole that swallowed Jeremy Martin up horns, hooves, and tail. It was like watching him run headfirst into eternal night.

With everyone else out of the way, Baal turned its attention toward Brian and Janet. It opened its mouth to roar, and all that came out was an unsettling child's giggle.

Brian grabbed his mother's hand and pulled her toward the tow truck. "Can you make it?" he asked.

"I'll try," Janet groaned, although it was clear she was struggling. Brian threw his mother's arm around his shoulders and tried to support her weight. Baal seemed to be in no hurry to kill them. Instead, he studied them with amusement, inhaling the essence of their fear.

They had taken no more than a couple of steps in the direction of the tow truck when they saw the faces of more minotaurs staring back at them from the woods—Leonard and Daisy's transformed minotaur faces. Brian's heart sank. The Order of the Bull had triumphed, and now they were emerging from the darkness to worship their god and sacrifice their lives. Everything was as good as finished.

Only that wasn't exactly right.

Brian's eyes widened as he saw the remaining members of The Sect of the Calf step into the light, holding the severed heads of the minotaurs high on stakes. Upon seeing Baal, the calf-men dropped the heads they'd been carrying and attacked. The ever-growing darkness that leaked out of Baal's fragile bovine shell immediately swallowed some of the sect up as it had done with Jeremy.

Unable to watch the proceedings, Brian used all of his strength and hauled his mother up into the passenger seat of the tow truck. "Just another minute," he said.

Brian climbed into the driver side of the vehicle, turned the key in the ignition, and sighed with relief as the tow truck rumbled to life. The truck's engine, however, was no match for the guttural noises of the bull-god which caused the glass windshield to vibrate and rattle in its frame.

Looking in his rearview mirror, Brian was surprised to see the remaining members of The Sect of the Calf armed, not with weapons, but with mirrors of their own.

The Sect of the Calf had the bull-god surrounded and were using their mirrors to show Baal his reflection. The god delighted in the pain and suffering of others but apparently despised seeing its own miserable state displayed in polished glass.

The bull bellowed and howled, making the kinds of sounds that might have been heard coming from the industrial ovens at Auschwitz.

As Brian put the truck in gear, it slowly inched forward, gliding over the carpet of pine needles. The Sect of the Calf had Baal effectively trapped, but they didn't know what to do with him from that point. One side of the creature was like a bottomless chasm of swirling black that he could drive the tow truck into and never find his way out of. The other flank was more or less intact, still gleaming just as brilliantly as the beer cans had on the day they were taken out of some redneck's ice chest.

Brian slowly angled the truck so that he was facing the aluminum side of the bull-god that still maintained some semblance of structure. He reached over and squeezed his mother's hand for support and slammed his foot down on the accelerator. The sect members scattered as the truck blazed across the clearing, slamming into the god before it could fully manifest into its true form. It was like watching a sledgehammer colliding with a block of ice. Bits of the creature flew everywhere, coating everything in a viscous gooey black sludge that had the consistency of motor oil and the smell of a slaughterhouse floor.

With the threat averted, the Sect of the Calf stared quietly at Baal's remains. No doubt, they were remembering that fateful night they pledged their blood and misery to the god, supplicating themselves in the hope of a better life. All they were given in reward for their dedication was madness, being held in a physical limbo that trapped them as part man, part cow. They had corrected their mistake today, but that did nothing to erase the bitter regrets they held for their foolishness.

The calf-men walked back into the forest without looking back...

Slowly Brian got out of the truck and walked cautiously over to what remained of Baal's skull. The flies that landed there, eager to lay their eggs, died within seconds. Brian took note of that and was careful not to touch anything.

He stared into the lifeless onyx eyes of the bull-god, searching for answers. In that blank stare he saw his father curled up in some dark place, grieving for all the things he had done wrong.

He also saw The Sect of the Calf as they had once been—humans worshiping dark divinity, hoping for better lives. Brian saw their past and the regret in their hearts. Their reward wasn't at all what they expected.

He watched in horror as the sect members danced and shouted and cut themselves. He watched them murder. He watched them change. Although he had seen all of it before, familiarity didn't make it any less riveting.

Something different, however, happened when they changed. Maybe they got Baal's attention much sooner than Uncle Jack's cult had. Or maybe they had botched an incantation. Whatever the case, they didn't revert to their human selves after transforming into the likeness of their god.

The change was enough to drive most of them mad, and chaos ensued.

Brian watched as desperate sect members ran through the trailer park, slamming their fists against the corrugated metal underpinnings, butting their heads against trees, running headlong into the trailers in hopes of breaking their necks and ending the misery. Baal wasn't that merciful. He wanted to see them suffer.

Some of the sect members ran through the forest frantically until they collapsed from exhaustion. Others ran toward Burton's Peak and threw themselves into the ravine. Some went back to the shack and cursed Baal in hopes of reversing the process.

These last remaining members of The Sect of the Calf were the ones who rallied against anything that might glorify Baal. These were the ones who had effectively helped to destroy the god who had destroyed them. Yet Baal was a very old being. Despite his temporary defeat, he most certainly wasn't dead.

It was enough to make Brian want to get as far away from this place as possible.

Somehow, he didn't think his mother would argue with him about moving anymore.

EPILOGUE

E lsewhere...
    The worst part about Hell is the remembering. Damnation offers no reprieve from the memories of bygone sins. Hell doesn't simply wipe the slate clean, but rather amplifies the recollections and half-memories, transforming them into full-blown mistakes that the mind has mercifully tried to repress.

The guilt that accompanies those memories is a ravenous beast that will devour you if you don't find a way to cage it. Some people use the trappings of religion to imprison their guilt. Others shackle it with alcohol. Some eliminate it entirely by staring down the barrel of a .45.

Jeremy had gone another route entirely, although he wasn't quite sure how to categorize it. Even as consciousness came rushing back, drawing his breath like a night-riding succubus, he knew where he was and why he was there. That knowledge, however, raised more questions than it answered.

The luminescent walls of the labyrinth glowed faintly in the darkness. And somewhere, deep within the depths of the maze, came the clip-clop of hooves on stone.

"Welcome home, brother," a voice whispered.

About The Author

Phillip Yates is the author of *The Order of the Bull*, *Bear Creek Massacre*, *The Devil Swims in the River Styx*, *The Deer Hunter*, and *Killer Shops For New Knife*. He is a two-time winner of the Lovecraft Cosmic Prize and was the 2021 nominee for The Blade's Horror Author of the Year award.

O	W	I	E	S	Y
E	A	W	P	F	T
L	R	H	K	M	L
S	N	T	O	K	E
Z	E	U	L	A	S
K	H	S	H	L	R